The Signalman

By Charles Dickens

Adapted by I. M. Richardson

Illustrated by Hal Ashmead

TROLL ASSOCIATES

Library of Congress Cataloging in Publication Data

Richardson, I. M.
 The signalman.

 (Famous tales of suspense)
 Summary: A signalman is visited by a ghostly
figure who seems to warn of approaching tragedies
along the railroad track.
 [1. Ghost—Fiction. 2. Railroads—Fiction]
I. Dickens, Charles, 1812-1870. The signal man.
II. Ashmead, Hal, ill. III. Title. IV. Series.
PZ7.R3948Si   [Fic]   81-19819
 ISBN 0-89375-630-X   AACR2
 ISBN 0-89375-631-8 (pbk.)

Printed in the United States of America
10 9 8 7 6 5 4 3 2 1

"Halloa! Below there!"

When he heard me calling down to him, he was standing near the signal house in front of the tunnel. A signal flag was in his hand, rolled around its short pole. I was on the cliff above him. But instead of looking up at me when I called, he looked down the tracks.

3

I called again, and this time he saw me. "I want to come down," I called. "Where is the path?" He looked at me without replying. Just then, the ground trembled, and a train roared past him. When I saw him again, he was rolling up the flag he had used to signal the engineer.

I asked again where the path was. He hesitated, then pointed
to a winding trail that led down from the top of the cliff to the
railroad tracks far below. I followed the path down and found
him standing between the rails. When I drew near, he stepped
back, as if he were afraid.

The signalman worked in a lonely, dreary place. On both sides of the tracks were high walls of jagged rock. They cut off the view of everything except a narrow strip of sky. In one direction, the tracks stretched out straight, then suddenly disappeared around a blind curve. In the other direction, they led into the gloomy mouth of the tunnel.

6

I explained to the signalman that I had seen him from the top of the cliff, and thought he might like a visitor. He glanced at the red warning light near the mouth of the tunnel, then looked back at me strangely.

"I thought I had seen you before," he said. "Over there—by the warning light."

I told him that I had never been there before, and he seemed more at ease. He told me about his duties—change that signal, trim those lights, turn this iron handle, listen for the electric bell. We went inside the signal house. There I saw a cozy fire, a desk at which he sat to make entries in an official book, and a telegraph key.

Our conversation was interrupted several times by the bell. Each time, the signalman read off messages or sent out replies. Once, he had to stand outside the door and wave a flag as a train passed. As he worked, he gave his full attention to each task. He was very alert, and worked very hard.

Twice, however, he turned pale and looked sharply at the bell when it did *not* ring. Then he opened the door and looked toward the red warning light at the mouth of the tunnel. He seemed upset.

"I am troubled, sir," he said at last. "If you will visit me again tomorrow night, I will tell you why."

We walked outside, and he said, "When you saw me, you
called out, '*Halloa! Below there*!' I know those words well. Did
they come to you in any supernatural way?"

"Not at all," I replied.

Then he asked me not to call out like that if I returned the
next night. I agreed and climbed back up the path.

The next night, I went to visit the signalman at eleven o'clock. I did not call out, but he was waiting for me at the bottom of the path, holding a lantern. We shook hands, then walked to the signal house and went inside.

"I took you for someone else yesterday," he said. "That troubles me."

"Who did you mistake me for?" I asked.

"I don't know," he replied. "I have never seen his face. His left arm is always across his face, and he frantically waves his right arm—like this."

I watched as he went through a motion that seemed to say, without actually using the words, *For God's sake, clear the way!*

"One moonlight night," explained the signalman, "I was sitting here, when I heard a voice cry, '*Halloa! Below there!*' I looked out and saw someone standing by the warning light near the tunnel, waving like I just showed you. The voice was hoarse from shouting, and it cried, '*Look out! Look out!*' And then it said again, '*Halloa! Below there! Look out! Look out!*'

"I turned my red lantern on and ran toward the figure, calling 'What's wrong? What has happened?' I came closer and reached out to pull its arm away from its eyes—but the figure was gone."

"You mean it had gone into the tunnel?" I said.

"No," he replied. "I ran into the tunnel and looked all around. It had disappeared.

"I climbed up the iron ladder to the top of the warning light and looked around," he said. "Then I came inside and telegraphed this message: *An alarm has been given. Is anything wrong?* The answer came back: *All is well. All is well.*"

"You must have imagined it," I said.

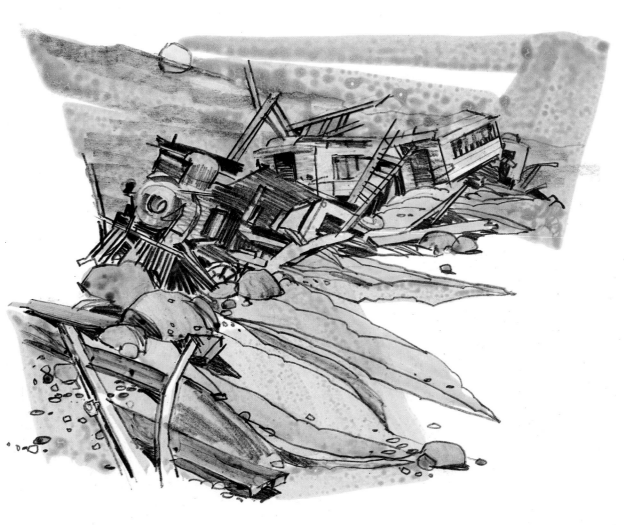

"Within six hours," he continued, "there was a horrible accident down the line. And within ten hours, the dead and injured were brought through the tunnel and over the very spot where the figure had stood."

A disagreeable shudder crept over me. The signalman laid his hand on my arm and glanced over his shoulder with hollow eyes. "This happened just a year ago," he added.

"Six or seven months passed," he said. "Then, early one morning, I looked towards the warning light and saw the specter again. This time, it did not cry out."

"Did it wave its arm?"

"No. Its hands covered its face, as if in mourning."

"Did you go up to it?" I asked.

"No," he replied. "I came inside and sat down, because I felt faint. When I looked out again, the figure was gone. But that very day, as a train came out of the tunnel, I saw something strange in the window of one of the passenger cars. It was a confusion of hands and heads—and something waved."

"I signaled the engineer to stop," said the signalman, "and he put the brakes on. The train traveled some distance farther. I ran after it, hearing terrible screams and cries. I learned that a beautiful young girl had suddenly died in one of the cars.

"She was brought in here and laid out on the floor," he added.

Without thinking, I pushed my chair back and looked from him to the floor, and back again.

"Now you can see why I am troubled," he said. "This specter came back a week ago. Since then, I have seen it by the warning light several times."

"What does it do?" I asked.

He replied, "It calls to me, '*Below there! Look out! Look out!*' It stands waving to me with one arm, while its other arm covers its eyes. It rings the bell."

"Did it ring the bell yesterday, when I was here?" I asked. "And did you then go to the door?"

"Yes," he replied. "Twice."

"Then see how your imagination misleads you," I said. "I was watching the bell and listening, and it did *not* ring at those times."

He shook his head and said, "I did not imagine it. You may not have heard it, but *I* did. And the ghost was out there when I looked—both times."

"Is it there now?" I asked.

He bit his lower lip, as if he were unwilling to look. We both stood up and went to the door. There was the warning light. There was the tunnel. There were the high stone walls on each side of the tracks.

"Do you see it?" I asked.

"No," he answered. "It is not there."

We sat down again. "What can it mean?" he asked. "What is the specter warning me about? There is danger somewhere on this line. Something dreadful is going to happen, I'm sure of that. But what? Where?" He pulled out a handkerchief and wiped his forehead.

He wiped the palms of his hands and said, "What warning could I send on the telegraph? Imagine what it would be like: 'Message: *Danger! Take care!* Answer: *What danger? Where?* Message: *Don't know. But take care!*' They would fire me. What else could they do?"

As the night passed, his duties demanded more and more of his attention, and he seemed to calm down a bit. I left him at two in the morning. But I kept thinking about the strange ghostlike figure he had described. I did not like it. I thought perhaps he should see a doctor and get a medical opinion.

The next day, when I looked down from the cliffs toward the railroad tracks, I was filled with horror. Near the tunnel was a figure whose left arm was across its eyes, and whose right arm was waving excitedly. Then I realized that it was not a ghost, but a man. He repeated the gesture again, apparently for a group of men a short distance away.

Something was wrong. I raced down the path as fast as I could.

"What is the matter?" I asked one of the men.

"The signalman was killed this morning, sir."

"Not the one who was on watch last night!" I cried.

He nodded and lifted the edge of a piece of canvas that covered the signalman's body.

"How did it happen?" I cried.

"He was cut down by an engine, sir. Somehow he was not clear of the tracks. It was just daylight. He still had his lamp in his hand. His back was toward the engine as it came out of the tunnel. The engineer was just showing us how it happened. Show the gentleman, Tom."

The engineer walked back toward the mouth of the tunnel, then turned to face me, and said, "I was coming round the curve in the tunnel, when I saw him. There was no time to slow down. He didn't seem to be paying any attention to the whistle. So I shut it off and called out to him as loud as I could."

"What did you say?" I asked.

"I said, '*Below there! Look out! For God's sake, clear the way!*'" replied the engineer. Then he added, "It was dreadful, sir. I could not bear to look. So I covered my eyes with this arm, and I waved this arm until the very last minute. And I kept calling, '*Below there! Look out! Look out!*'"